Step into Reading®

MARC BROWN

Step into Reading® Books

Random House New York

Copyright © 2001 by Marc Brown. All rights reserved under International and Pan-American Copyright Conventions. Published in the United States by Random House, Inc., New York, and simultaneously in Canada by Random House of Canada Limited, Toronto.

www.randomhouse.com/kids

Library of Congress Cataloging-in-Publication Data
Brown, Marc Tolon. Arthur's hiccups / Marc Brown. p. cm. "Step into reading books."
SUMMARY: When Arthur gets the hiccups, his family and friends try everything they can think of to make them go away.
ISBN 0-375-80698-9 (trade) — ISBN 0-375-90698-3 (lib. bdg.)
[1. Hiccups—Fiction. 2. Aardvark—Fiction.] I. Title.
PZ7.B81618Aqb 2001 [E]—dc21 00-045725
Printed in the United States of America September 2001 10 9 8 7 6 5 4 3 2 1

STEP INTO READING, RANDOM HOUSE, and the Random House colophon are registered trademarks and the Step into Reading colophon is a trademark of Random House, Inc.
ARTHUR is a registered trademark of Marc Brown.

"Don't eat your cake so fast,"
said Arthur's mother.
"You'll get the—"
"Hic," said Arthur. "Hic, hic."
D.W. giggled.

"Arthur's got the hiccups,
    Arthur's got the hiccups,"
she laughed.
"It's not—hic—funny,"
said Arthur.

"Drink a glass of water,"

said his mother.

So he did.

But still he had the hiccups.

"Hold your breath
and count to twenty,"
said his father.
So he did.
But still he had the hiccups.

"I know how to get rid
of your hiccups," said D.W.

"I don't—hic—need your help,"
said Arthur.

"My friend the Brain
will—hic—know."

Arthur ran to the telephone
and called the Brain.

"Hiccups can be serious,"
the Brain told Arthur.
"I read in my Book of Records
about an old man who had
hiccups for three years."

"Three years!" said Arthur.

"Wow, what happened to him?"

"He died," said the Brain.

"But don't worry,"
said the Brain.
"You can get rid of them
by standing on your head
for five minutes."

So Arthur stood on his head.

But every time he hiccuped,

he fell over.

"This is more fun than television!"

laughed D.W.

"Maybe Buster can help,"

said Arthur.

Buster came right away
to Arthur's house.
He brought his big joke book.
"A good laugh can cure anything,"
said Buster.
"Here's a funny one:

'What's smaller than an elephant,
more annoying than a mosquito,
and never goes away?'"

"I—hic—don't know," said Arthur.

"'Your sister!'" said Buster.

Arthur fell down laughing.

"Not funny," said D.W.

"Is—hic—too," said Arthur.

"Well, I did my best," said Buster.

"So long and good luck."

Soon the bell rang again.

It was Muffy and Francine.

"We came to cure you," said Muffy.

"This lollipop will do it,"

said Francine. "Follow us."

"The key is to lick it

while hanging upside down,"

said Francine.

"It's an old family cure,"

said Muffy. "Works every time."

Arthur hung from the swing

for a long time.

Muffy looked at her watch.

"Just one more minute," she said.

"Keep licking," said Francine.

No one said a word.

"I think they're gone!"

whispered D.W.

"Hic!" said Arthur,

louder than ever.

Arthur hiccuped
through his homework.

He hiccuped
while he brushed his teeth.

"Are you sure you don't want
   my help?" asked D.W.
"You can't—hic—help me,"
   Arthur said. "No one can."

Arthur was still hiccuping
when he climbed into bed.
Suddenly something from
under the bed grabbed his leg.

Arthur screamed.

D.W. laughed.

"I'll get you for this, D.W.!"
yelled Arthur.

D.W. laughed and laughed.

"Hey!" said Arthur. "They're gone!
You scared my hiccups away.
Thanks, D.W."

But D.W. was laughing so hard
all she could say was
"You're—hic—welcome!"